MaMa Goose
Rhymes and Poems for the Little Ones

A Collection by Edelen Wille

Edited by Frances Edelen Clegg
and Cheryl Wille Clegg

Andrews McMeel
Publishing

Kansas City

www.edelenwille.com

Library of Congress Cataloging-in-Publication Data

MaMa Goose : rhymes and poems for the little ones : a collection / by Edelen Wille ; edited by Frances Edelen Clegg and Cheryl Wille Clegg.
    p. cm.
  Summary: An illustrated collection of favorite nursery rhymes and poems, including some finger plays, games, and songs.
  ISBN: 0-7407-3130-0
  1. Nursery rhymes. 2. Children's poetry. [1. Nursery rhymes.] I. Clegg, Frances Edelen.
II. Clegg, Cheryl Wille. III. Edelen Wille.

PZ8.3.M3 106 2003

2003048103

03 04 05 06 07 ELP 10 9 8 7 6 5 4 3 2 1

Design by Frances Edelen Clegg and Cheryl Wille Clegg
Project editor: Marti Petty
Production: Elizabeth Nuelle

ATTENTION: SCHOOLS AND BUSINESSES
Andrews McMeel books are available at quantity discounts with bulk purchase for educational, business, or sales promotional use. For information, please write to: Special Sales Department, Andrews McMeel Publishing, 4520 Main Street, Kansas City, Missouri 64111.

Dedicated to Walker, Annabelle, Hadley, Madeline and Charlie.
Our rhyme and reason.

A Letter from Edelen Wille

"Great A, little a, over the hills and far away.
Old King Cole and The Queen of Hearts,
Rub-a-dub-dub and the Twinkling Stars . . ."

What makes these ancient rhymes made of such whimsy and nonsense so unforgettable and so important to children everywhere? Most Mother Goose rhymes have been handed down through centuries by French, English, Irish, Scottish and American mothers and fathers. Magically their lyrical beat has echoed through generations.

Many a great editor and illustrator have taken their turn with this goosey gal; we hope our compilation will add another sweet note in this timeless symphony of enchanted poetry.

Weaving a tapestry of rich vintage fabrics, best loved children's illustrators and our favorite rhymes, we have tried to make a patchwork that represents this capricious story. The outcome is hopefully something to share with the littlest in age and the youngest at heart.

To borrow a thought from one of the greater poets:
"We may wander from home as far as we will,
But the songs of our childhood will sing to us still."
With full and humble hearts we introduce,
this newest collection we call MaMa Goose.

Cheryl Wille Cleer

Frances Edelen

GIRLS and boys come out to play,
   the moon doth shine as bright as day;

Leave your supper and leave your sleep,
   And come with your playfellows into the street.

Come with a whoop, come with a call,
   Come with a good will or not at all.

Up the ladder and down the wall,
   A halfpenny roll will serve us all.

You find milk and I'll find flour,
   And we'll have pudding in half an hour.

LITTLE boy blue,
  come blow your horn,
The sheep's in the meadow,
  the cow's in the corn;
But where's the little boy
  who looks after the sheep?
He's under the haystack,
  fast asleep.
Will you wake him?
  No, not I,
For if I do, he'll be
  sure to cry.

To market, to market,
to buy a plum cake,
Home again, home again,
market is late;
To market, to market,
to buy a plum bun,
Home again, home again,
market is done.

TWINKLE, twinkle, little star,
How I wonder what you are!
Up above the world so high,
Like a diamond in the sky.

When the blazing sun is gone,
When he nothing shines upon,
Then you show your little light,
Twinkle, twinkle, all the night.

When the traveler in the dark
Thanks you for your tiny spark:
How could he see where to go
If you did not twinkle so?

THERE was an old woman tossed
    in a blanket
Seventeen times as high as the moon;
But where she was going no mortal
    could tell,
For under her arm she carried a broom.

Old woman, old woman, old woman,
    said I,
Whither, ah whither, ah whither so high?
To sweep the cobwebs from the sky,
And I'll be with you
    by and by.

13

SAID THIS LITTLE FAIRY

Said this little fairy, "I'm as thirsty as can be."
Said this little fairy, "I'm hungry, too, dear me!"
Said this little fairy, "Who'll tell us where to go?"
Said this little fairy, "I'm sure that I don't know."
Said this little fairy, "Let's brew some dewdrop tea."
So they sipped it and ate honey beneath the maple tree.

A BURROWING GAME

See the little mousie, creeping up the stair,
Looking for a warm nest—there, oh, there!

(Mother's fingers creep up the body, and finally fumble in baby's neck.)

PAT A CAKE

A Froebel Finger Play

Baby, would you like to make
For yourself a little cake?
Pat it gently, smooth it down.
Baker says: "Now, in to brown;
Bring it here, baby dear,
While the oven fire burns clear."
"Baker, see, here is my cake;
Bake it well for baby's sake."
"In the oven, right deep down,
Here the cake will soon get brown."

A KNEE GAME

What do I see? Baby's knee.
Tickily, tickily, tic, tac, tee.
One for a penny, two for a pound;
Tickily, tickily, round and round.

A FOOT PLAY

Up, down—up, down.
One foot up and one foot down,
All the way to London town.
Tra la la la la la.

15

Little girl, Little girl

"Little girl, little girl,
  where have you been?"
"Gathering roses to
  give to the Queen."

"Little girl, little girl,
  what gave she you?"
"She gave me a diamond
  as big as my shoe."

16

There Was a Crooked Man

There was a crooked man and
he went a crooked mile,
He found a crooked sixpence
upon a crooked stile.

He bought a crooked cat which
caught a crooked mouse,
And they all lived together
in a little crooked house.

Why?

Do you know why moo cows moo?

Or why little pigs go woo-woo?

Or why bunnies cannot talk

Just as well as doggies walk?

Or why we get very hungry

When there's nothing 'round to eat?

Or why fuzzy little ducklings

Have such funny-looking feet?

Or why it is that pigeons coo

And roosters crow cockle-doodle-doo?

And why's the ocean salty

And lakes not salt a bit?

Awful curious, ain't it,

When you stop to

      think of it?

Mary, Mary quite contrary,
How does your garden grow?

With silver bells and cockleshells,
And pretty maids all in a row.

Ring around the rosies, a pocket full of posies
Ashes, ashes, we all fall down!

The cows are in the meadow, eating yellow buttercups
Thunder, lightning, we all get up!

PEASE-porridge hot,
Pease-porridge cold,
Pease-porridge in the pot
nine days old.
Some like it hot,
Some like it cold,
Some like it in the pot
nine days old.

The Rainbow

A glorious rainbow I saw one day,
And of what do you s'pose it was made?

Soft misty veils that the rain had spun
And the sun had painted EVERY shade!

As the clouds scurried off and waved good-bye
The wind whispered softly:
"A sash for the sky!"

THE Queen of Hearts
She made some tarts,
All on a summer's day.

The Knave of Hearts,
He stole the tarts,
And took them
clean away.

CURLY locks! Curly locks!
wilt thou be mine?
Thou shall not wash dishes,
nor yet feed the swine;
But sit on a cushion and
sew a fine seam,
And feed upon
strawberries,
sugar, and
cream!

HANDY Spandy,
Jack a-dandy,
Loves plum-cake and
sugar candy;
He bought some at
a grocer's shop,
And out he came,
hop-hop-hop.

DING, dong bell,
  Pussy's in the well!

Who put her in?
  Little Johnny Green;

Who pulled her out,
  Big Tom Stout.

I Saw Three Ships Come Sailing By

I saw three ships come sailing by, sailing by, sailing by;
I saw three ships come sailing by on
New Year's Day in the morning.

I saw three ships come sailing by, sailing by, sailing by;
I saw three ships come sailing by
and what do you think was in them then.

I saw three ships come sailing by, sailing by, sailing by;
I saw three ships come sailing by and three
pretty girls were in them then.

And one could whistle, and once could sing,
The other could play on the violin;
Such joy there was at my wedding
On New Year's Day in the morning.

One, two, three, four,
  Mary's at the cottage door,
Five, six, seven, eight,
  Eating cherries off a plate.

Old King Cole

Old King Cole was a merry old soul,
     and a merry old soul was he;
and he called for his pipe, and he called for his bowl,
     and he called for his fiddlers three.

Ev'ry fiddler had a fiddle fine,
     a very fine fiddle had he;
then tweedle-dee went the fiddlers three,
     and so merry we will be.

37

BOSSY-COW,
bossy-cow,
where do you lie?
In the green meadow
under the sky.

BILLY GOAT,
billy goat,

where do you lie?

In the shed by the stable

till morning

comes by.

BIRDIES BRIGHT,
birdies bright,
where do you lie?

Up in the

tree tops,

oh, ever so high!

JOHNNY-HORSE,

Johnny-horse,
where do you lie?
Out in the stable
with nobody nigh.

CACKLE-HEN,

cackle-hen,

where do you lie?

I lie in the

hen house

with chickies

close by.

DONKEY,
oh donkey,
where do you lie?
In the barnyard
by the stable
till rooster's
first cry.

48

BABY SWEET,
baby sweet,
where do you lie?
In the warm straw
with doggie close by.

BOBBY Shaftoe's gone to sea,
  Silver buckles on his knee;
He'll come back and marry me,
  Pretty Bobby Shaftoe.

Bobby Shaftoe's fit and fair,
  Combing down his yellow hair;
He's my love for evermore;
  Pretty Bobby Shaftoe.

Ella Dolbear Lee

HUMPTY Dumpty
sat on a wall,
Humpty Dumpty
had a great fall;

All the king's horses and
all the king's men,
Couldn't put Humpty
Dumpty together
again.

PUSSY CAT, pussy cat, where have you been?
I've been up to London to look at the queen.
Pussy cat, pussy cat, what did you there?
I frightened a little mouse under the chair.

PETER, Peter, pumpkin-eater;
    Had a wife, and couldn't keep her;
He put her in a pumpkin shell,
    And there he kept her very well.

MY LITTLE GARDEN

1. See my little garden,

2. How I rake it over,

3. Then I sow the little brown seeds,

4. And with soft earth cover.

5. Now the raindrops patter
   On the earth so gaily;

6. See the big round sun smile
   On my garden daily.

7. The little plant is waking;
   Down the roots grow creeping;

8. Up now come the leaflets
   Through the brown
   earth peeping.

9. Soon the buds will laugh up
   Toward the springtime showers;
   Soon my buds will open
   Into happy flowers.

THERE was a little girl,
Who wore a little curl,
Between her two eyes of blue.

When she was glad,
She was very, very glad,
And when she was sad,
cried "Boo-hoo!"

DOODLE Doodle Doo,
   The Princess lost her shoe;
Her Highness hopped—
   the fiddler stopped,
Not knowing what to do.

HEY diddle diddle
the cat and the fiddle,
The cow jumped
over the moon;
The little dog laughed
to see such sport,
And the dish ran away
with the spoon.

ROCK-a-Bye, baby,
　　thy cradle is green;
Father's a nobleman,
　　mother's a queen;
And Betty's a lady,
　　and wears a gold ring;
And Johnny's a drummer,
　　and drums for the king.

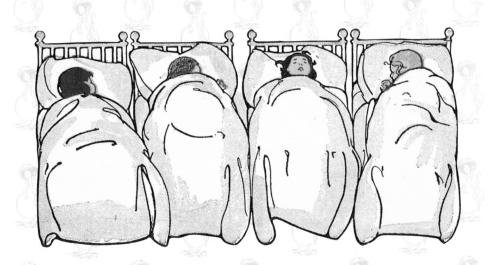

Ship ahoy!
　Ship ahoy!
"What is the name
　Of your ship, my boy?"

"Her name," said he,
　Is the *Annabelle Lee,*
The smartest craft
　Upon the sea;
And I am the skipper
　As you can see."

Ship ahoy!
　Ship ahoy!
"Your pardon, cap'n,"
　Says I to the boy.

"And Polly's the mate
　Of the *Annabelle Lee,*
And also the cook,
　And the crew," said he.
"We're taking our doggie
　On a trip to sea,
He's fond of the water,
　As you can see."

66

Lavender's Blue

LAVENDER'S blue, dilly, dilly!
    Lavender's green;
When I am King dilly, dilly!
    You shall be Queen.

Call up your men, dilly, dilly!
    Set them to work,
Some to the plough, dilly, dilly!
    Some to the cart.

Some to make hay, dilly, dilly!
    Some to cut corn;
While you and I, dilly, dilly!
    Keep ourselves warm.

69

Little Jumping Joan

HERE am I,
little jumping Joan,
when nobody's with me
I'm always alone.

NAMING THE FINGERS

THIS is little Tommy Thumb,
Round and smooth as any plum.
This is busy Peter Pointer:
Surely he's a double-jointer.
This is mighty Toby Tall:
He's the biggest one of all.
This is dainty Reuben Ring:
He's too fine for anything.
And this little wee one, maybe,
Is the pretty Finger-baby.

All the five we've counted now,
Busy fingers in a row.
Every finger knows the way
How to work and how to play;
Yet together they work best,
Each one helping all the rest.

Baby Dear

WHERE did you come from, baby dear?
Out of the everywhere into here.

Where did you get those eyes of blue?
Out of the sky as I came through.

What makes the light in them sparkle and spin?
Some of the starry twinkles left in.

But how did you come to us, you dear?
God thought about you, and so I am here.

In Springtime, all the small
boys shout:
"Hurrah, come bring your
marbles out."

Summer days are here again;
Through the sunny
hours,
In the meadow, Polly Anne,
Gathers fragrant flowers.

Autumn time is harvest time;
　　Apples ripe are falling,
Lying thick upon the ground;
　　And the bluejays calling.

AUTUMN

I was a snowball;
　　I grew and grew,
Now I am a
　　Snowman;
How do you do?

Winter is jolly
　　With ice and snow;
But when it gets warm
　　I have to go.

WINTER

Lillian Sturges

Seesaw Margery Daw,
  Jacky shall have a new master;

Jacky must have but a penny a day,
  Because he can work no faster.

See, saw, sacaradown, sacaradown,
Which is the way to London town?

One foot up, and the other foot down,
That is the way to London town.

Three Mice Went Into a Hole to Spin

THREE mice went into a hole
  to spin;
Puss passed by, and Puss looked in;
"What are you doing, my little men?"
"Weaving coats for Gentlemen."
"Please let me help you to wind off
  your threads,"
"Ah, no, Mistress Pussy, you'd chase
  us instead!
Ah, no, Mistress Pussy, you'd chase
  us instead!

THE WAVELETS' INVITATION

Playful little wavelets
 Crept 'long the shore one day,
Till they found a cozy spot
 Where they could stay and play.
Then they invited little children
 To come down and gather shells
And listen to the wondrous story
 That the good Sea Fairy tells.

The Little Searchlight

Flash, little searchlight!
   Flash and glow!
Are you Wake-a-by-King
   On the earth here below?

Do you watch tiny tots
   On their soft downy pillow
As they niddy-nod
   On hush-a-by billow?

Or are you a firefly,
   Golden with light,
Swinging your lantern
   To brighten the night?

Can little children
   Play tag with you?
Or leap frog, or hide,
   Or just peek-a-boo?

Whatever you are
   You're a beautiful bug!
If you weren't so tiny
   We'd give you a hug!

84

Putting the Fingers to Sleep

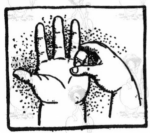

MY fingers are so sleepy,
　　It's time they went to bed.
So first, you Baby Finger
　　Tuck in your little head.

Ringman, come, now it's your turn,
　　And then come, Tallman Great;
Now, Pointer Finger, hurry
　　Because it's getting late.

Let's see if all are snuggled.
　　No, here's one more to come,
So come, lie close, little brothers,
　　Make room for Master Thumb.

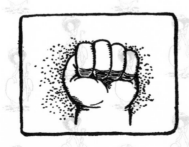

Faithful Little Farmers

There's a little band of farmers—
  Some of them I know—
Who are working 'round the country,
  And not one can use a hoe!

But that fact doesn't matter—
  Each works with might and main
From early morn till evening,
  In sunshine or in rain.

Today I saw them working,
  Working very hard;
Some were in the meadow,
  Some out in the yard.

They swallow up the beetles
  That kill the grain and trees,
They eat the bugs and insects
  That ruin corn and peas.

Each farmer is a singer—
  Of this I am quite sure.
Let's ask them all to linger,
  So insects may be fewer.

And now about these workers—
  I wonder if you've heard
That every singing farmer
  Is just a little bird?

Two Little Hands

TWO little hands so soft and white,
This is the left—this is the right.
Five little fingers stand on each,
So I can hold a plum or a peach.
But if I should grow as old as you
Lots of little things these hands can do.

OVER the river and through
		the woods,
To grandmother's house we go;
The horse knows the way
		To carry the sleigh,
Through the white and drifting snow.

Over the river and through
		the woods,
Oh how the wind does blow!
It stings the toes and bites the nose
		As over the ground we go.

MY BALL
OF TWINE

MY ball of twine is red and strong,

It makes me think of

Christmas song

And many candles blowing,

It ties my gifts, both round and flat,

First up and down,

this way and that,

And loves to start them going.

Old Father Santa Claus

WHEN the nursemaid put out the light,
These two little people dressed in white
Rolled themselves up in the counterpane,
And did not dare to look out again.

But when the bells were ringing ding-dong,
Old Father Santa Claus passed along;
"Whish," he said, brushing the snow from his nose,
"Whew! how the east wind blusters and blows."

Then through the window he spied the bed;
"I have to call at this house," he said;
"The chimney's the proper way for me,
Why are they built so narrow?" said he.

In at the window he went instead—
Seated himself at the foot of the bed—
Filled the stocking with sweetmeats and toys—
All without making the slightest noise.

Now wake little children dressed in white,
Old Father Santa Claus came last night;
He stuffed your stocking—and children, look!
He brought you a colored picture book.

Over the Hills and Far Away

Tom he was a piper's son,
    he learnt to play when he was young;
but all the tune that he could play, was
    "Over the hills and far away."
Over the hills and a great way off
    the wind shall blow my top-knot off!

Tom with his pipe made such a noise
    That he pleased both the girls and boys.
And so they stopped to hear him play
    "Over the hills and far away."

Dance to Your Daddy

Dance to your daddy my little laddie!
Dance to your daddy my little lamb!
You shall have a fishy on a little dishy,
you shall have a fishy when
the boat comes in!

Dance to your daddy my little babby!
Dance to your daddy my little lamb!

Oh! Dear, What Can the Matter Be?

Oh! dear, what can the matter be?
Oh! dear, what can the matter be?
Oh! dear, what can the matter be?
Johnny's so long at the fair.

He promised to bring me a basket of posies,
a garland of lilies, a garland of roses.
He promised to bring me a bunch of blue
ribbons to tie up my bonny brown hair.

Simple Simon

Simple Simon met a pieman
going to the fair;
said Simple Simon to the pieman
"Let me taste your ware."

Said the pieman unto Simon
"Show me first your penny,"
said Simple Simon to the pieman
"Indeed, I have not any."

As Tommy Snooks and
Bessy Brooks
Were walking out one Sunday,
Said Tommy Snooks to
Bessy Brooks,
"Will you marry me
on Monday?"

POLLY, put the kettle on,
Polly, put the kettle on,
Polly, put the kettle on,
We'll all have tea.

Sukey, take it off again,
Sukey, take it off again,
Sukey, take it off again,
They've all gone away.

MARY had a little lamb
Its fleece was white as snow,
And everywhere that Mary went
The lamb was sure to go.

It followed her to school one day,
Which was against the rule;
It made the children laugh and play,
To see a lamb at school.

And so the teacher turned it out,
But still it lingered near,
And waited patiently about
Till Mary did appear.

"Why does the lamb love Mary so?"
The eager children cry.
"Why, Mary loves the lamb, you know!"
The teacher did reply.

TROT, TROT, THE BABY GOES

Every evening Baby goes
Trot, trot, to town—
Across the river, through the fields,
Up hill and down.

Trot, trot, the Baby goes,
Up hill and down,
To buy a feather for her hat,
To buy a woolen gown.

Trot, trot, the Baby goes;
The birds fly down, alack!
"You cannot have our feathers, dear,"
They say; "So please trot back."

Trot, trot, the Baby goes;
The lambs come bleating near.
"You cannot have our wool," they say;
"But we are sorry, dear."

Trot, trot, the Baby goes,
Trot, trot, to town.
She buys a red rose for her hat,
She buys a cotton gown.

UP TO THE CEILING

Up to the ceiling, down to the ground,
Backward and forward, round and round;
Dance, little baby, and mother will sing,
With the merry chorus, ding, ding, ding!

THIS IS THE WAY

This is the way the ladies ride,
Nin! Nin! Nin!
This is the way the gentlemen ride,
Trot! Trot! Trot!
This is the way the farmers ride,
Jogglety! Jogglety! Jogglety! Jog!

RIDE A COCK-HORSE

Ride a cock-horse to Charing Cross,
To see a young lady jump on a white horse,
With rings on her fingers, and bells on her toes,
She shall have music wherever she goes.

Seesaw Margery Daw

Seesaw Margery Daw,
   Jacky shall have a new master;

Jacky must have but a penny a day,
   Because he can work no faster.

110

The North Wind Does Blow

The North Wind does blow
and we shall have snow;
and what will the Robin do,
the poor thing?

He'll sit in the barn
to keep himself warm,
and hide his head under his wing,
poor thing!

LITTLE Jack Horner
sat in a corner
Eating a Christmas pie;
He put in his thumb,
and pulled out a plum,
And said,
"What a good
boy am I!"

One and One

TWO little girls are better than one,
Two little boys can double the fun,
Two little birds can build a fine nest,
Two little arms can love mother best.
Two little ponies must go to a span;
Two little pockets has my little man;
Two little eyes to open and close,
Two little ears and one little nose,
Two little elbows, dimpled and sweet,
Two little shoes on two little feet,
Two little lips and one little chin,
Two little cheeks with a rose shut in;
Two little shoulders, chubby and strong,
Two little legs running all day long.
Two little prayers does my darling say,
Twice does he kneel by my side each day.

Three Face Plays

BROW BENDER

Brow bender,
Eye peeper,
Nose smeller,
Mouth eater,
Chin chopper,
Knock at the door—peep in,
Lift up the latch—walk in.

EYE WINKER

Eye winker,
Tom Tinker,
Nose smeller,
Mouth eater,
Chin chopper,
Chin chopper.

HERE SITS THE LORD MAYOR

Here sits the Lord Mayor,
Here sit his two men;
Here sits the cock,
And here sits the hen.

Here sit the chickens,
And here they go in;
Chippety, chippety,
Chippety chin.

Two Foot Plays

THIS LITTLE PIG

This little pig went to market;
This little pig stayed at home;
This little pig had roast beef;
This little pig had none;
And this little pig cried,
    "Wee, wee, wee!"
All the way home.

SHOE THE OLD HORSE

Shoe the old horse,
    Shoe the old mare;
But let the colt
    Go bare, bare, bare.

LITTLE acts of kindness,
  Like a summer flower,
Brighten many a weary face,
  Soothe a lonely hour.

Hearts can carry sorrow,
  Faces can look sad:
We can bring them sunshine.
  We can make them glad.

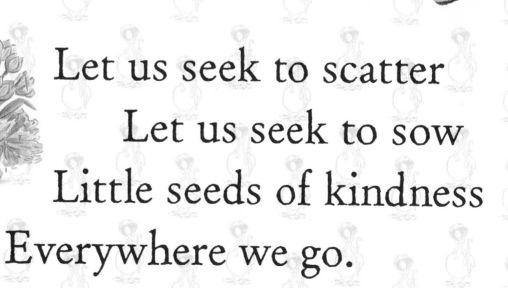

Let us seek to scatter
  Let us seek to sow
Little seeds of kindness
Everywhere we go.

Merry are the Bells

Merry are the bells, and merry
   would they ring,
Merry was myself, and merry could I sing;
With a merry ding-dong,
      happy, gay, and free,
And a merry sing-song, happy let us be!

Merry have we met,
      and merry have we been,
Merry let us part, and merry meet again;
With our merry sing-song,
      happy, gay, and free,
And a merry ding-dong, happy let us be!

Little Bo-Peep has lost her sheep,
And can't tell where to find them.

Leave them alone, and they'll come home,
Wagging their tails behind them.

Hush-a-bye, baby, on the tree top
  When the wind blows, the cradle will rock;

When the bough bends, the cradle may fall
  Down will come baby, cradle and all.

HUSH, baby, my doll,
I pray you, don't cry,
And I'll give you some bread,
and some milk

By-and-by;
Or, perhaps, you like custard,
or, maybe, a tart;
Then to either you
are welcome,
with all my heart.

COCK crows in
the morn
to tell us to rise,
And he who lies late will
never be wise;
For early to bed, and early
to rise,
Is the way to be
healthy and wealthy
and wise.

JACK and Jill went up the hill,
  To fetch a pail of water;
Jack fell down and broke his crown,
  And Jill came tumbling after.

Up Jack got and home did trot,
  As fast as he could caper;
Dame Jill had the job to plaster his knob,
  With vinegar and brown paper.

DEEDLE, deedle, dumpling,
my son John,
He went to bed with his
stockings on,
One shoe off, and one shoe on,
Deedle, deedle, dumpling,
my son John.

RUB-a-dub-dub,
   Three men in a tub,
And who do you think they be?
The butcher, the baker,
   The candlestick-maker;
turn'em out knaves all three.

Commandments for Parties

EVERY time before I go
To a party, dressed just so,

Mother, in her rocking-chair,
Smooths my frock and pats my hair,

Straightens every bit of lace,
Sees that every curl's in place,

Pins my gold-and-garnet pin,
Ties a bow beneath my chin,

Gives my nose a pair of tweaks,
Kisses me on both my cheeks;

Then she says, "Now, don't forget;
Be a little lady, Pet.

"When your little friends you see,
Drop a curtsy, prettily;

Play with them; but, honey-child,
Do not shout and don't be wild;

"Do not romp and do not tease,
Do your very best to please.

"At the table, sit up straight,
Keep your fingers from your plate.

"Use your fork, and do not take
Twice of ice cream or of cake.

"Do not soil your pretty frock;
come right home at four o'clock.

"When it's time to say good-bye,
don't be awkward, don't be shy;

"Smile, and don't forget to add
What a lovely time you've had,—

"Darling! *Please* don't twist your hat!"
Gracious! Where's the fun in *that!*

Little Tom Tucker

Little Tom Tucker sings for his supper;
what shall we give him?
White bread and butter.

How can he cut it without e'er a knife?
How can he marry without e'er a wife?

I Had a Little Nut-Tree

I had a little nut-tree nothing would it bear
but a silver nutmeg and a golden pear.

The King of Spain's daughter came to visit me
and all for the sake of my little nut-tree.

Sweet and Low

By Alfred, Lord Tennyson

SWEET and low, sweet and low,
Wind of the western sea.
Low, low, breathe and blow,
Wind of the western sea!
Over the rolling waters go,
Come from the dying moon, and blow,
Blow him again to me;
While my little one,
       while my pretty one, sleeps.

Sleep and rest, sleep and rest,
Father will come to thee soon;
Rest, rest, on Mother's breast,
Father will come to thee soon;
Father will come to his Babe in the Nest,
Silver sails all out of the West
Under the Silver Moon;
Sleep, my little one, sleep,
       my pretty one, sleep.

PAT-a-cake, pat-a-cake,
baker's man!
Bake me a cake
as fast as you can:
Pat it and prick it,
and mark it with B,
Put it in the oven
for Baby and me.

HERE we go round the mulberry bush,
The mulberry bush, the mulberry bush,
Here we go round the mulberry bush,
On a cold and frosty morning.

This is the way we wash our hands,
Wash our hands, wash our hands,
This is the way we wash our hands,
On a cold and frosty morning.

This is the way we wash our clothes,
Wash our clothes, wash our clothes,
This is the way we wash our clothes,
On a cold and frosty morning.

WASH the dishes,
Wipe the dishes,

Ring the bell for tea;
Three good wishes,
Three good kisses,
I will give to thee.

Little Miss Muffet
   Sat on a tuffet,
Eating some curds and whey.

Along came a spider,
      And sat down beside her,
And frightened Miss Muffet away.

146

There was an old woman who lived in a shoe,
She had so many children,
    she didn't know what to do.

She gave them some broth without any bread,
She kissed them all sweetly
    and put them to bed.

HICKORY, dickory, dock,
The mouse ran up the clock,
The clock struck one,
The mouse ran down;
Hickory, dickory, dock.

SPRING is coming, spring is coming,
Birdies, build your nest;
Weave together straw and feather,
Doing each your best.

Spring is coming, spring is coming,
Flowers are coming too:
Pansies, lilies, daffodillies
Now are coming through.

Spring is coming, spring is coming,
All around is fair:
Shimmer and quiver on the river,
Joy is everywhere.

Lazy Sheep, Pray Tell Me Why?

Lazy sheep, pray tell me why
    in the pleasant field you lie,
eating grass and daisies white
    From the morning till the night?
Ev'rything can something do,
    but what kind of use are you?

"Nay, my little master, nay,
    do not serve me so, I pray;
don't you see the wool that grows
    On my back to make your clothes?
Cold, ah, very cold you'd be
If you had not wool from me."

153

Peek-a-Boo Moon

A bunch of fluffy clouds one day
Decided just at noon
'Twould be the jolliest of sport
To play "Hide" with Miss Moon.

So they invited Mist and Fog,
Who were romping in the air,
And pretty soon they sailed away
Toward Miss Moon's starry lair.

My! Oh, they had to hurry though,
Miss Moon lived far away!
And when Miss Night Time came along
They had a glorious play!

We watched them as they raced, for we
Knew what they planned to do;
While Mist and Fog played hide-and-seek
Miss Moon played peek-a-boo!

The Sleepy Song

AS soon as the fire burns red and low
And the house upstairs is still,
She sings me a queer little sleepy song,
Of sheep that go over the hill.

The good little sheep run quick and soft,
Their colours are gray and white:
They follow their leader nose to tail,
For they must be home by night.

And one slips over and one comes next,
And one runs after behind,
The gray one's nose at the white one's tail,
The top of the hill they find.

And when they get to the top of the hill
They quietly slip away,
But one runs over and one comes next—
Their colours are white and gray.

And over they go, and over they go,
And over the top of the hill,
The good little sheep run thick and fast,
And the house upstairs is still.

And one slips over and one comes next,
The good little, gray little sheep!
I watch how the fire burns red and low,
And she says that I fall asleep.

NURSERY · RHYMES

Nursery Rhymes cont.

Art Index